HADDOCK

For Hannah Louise Smith
J.M.

For Juliette
F.M.

Text copyright © 1994 Jan Mark
Illustrations copyright © 1994 Fiona Moodie

First published in Great Britain in 1994
by Simon & Schuster Young Books
Campus 400
Maylands Avenue
Hemel Hempstead
Herts HP2 7EZ

Typeset in 15/22 Sabon by Goodfellow & Egan Ltd, Cambridge
Printed and bound in Belgium by Proost International Book Productions

British Library Cataloguing in Publication Data available.

ISBN: 0 7500 1444 X
ISBN: 0 7500 1445 8

HADDOCK

Jan Mark

Illustrated by Fiona Moodie

SIMON & SCHUSTER
YOUNG BOOKS

There was once a haddock who fell in love with a mermaid.
He gave her fishy gifts and followed her everywhere, from
the depths to the shallows, but there were places where
even a haddock could not go.

For the mermaid liked to sit upon a rock and make
eyes at passing fishermen. The haddock could only
bob alongside and blow devoted bubbles.
"O come with me to the bottom of the sea,"
the haddock sang.
"Stick to your own kind," the mermaid said,
while the scales on her tail clinked scornfully.
"But you are my kind," the haddock said,
and sank below the surface.

The mermaid hoped to marry a mortal man
and live upon land, but from where the haddock
was looking, she was all fish.
Every day the mermaid sang to the fishermen,
but the fishermen put limpets in their ears and
rowed rapidly away from the mermaid.
Their mothers had warned them about girls
like her.

There was one fisherman whose mother had run off to live in a lighthouse, so he had no one to give him good advice. His name was Stanley. When he heard the mermaid singing he steered close to the rock.

"Nice weather we're having," Stanley said. The mermaid smiled and all the scales on her tail chimed harmoniously.
After that, Stanley came back every day.

"Take me home with you, Stanley, and make me
your fishwife," the mermaid said, twirling her tail.
"There are ten steps up to the front door," said
Stanley, and he looked at the tail.
"I'll sing to you all day, Stanley," the mermaid
said, and she began to sing there and
then, upon the rock.
Stanley wondered what
the neighbours
would say.

Night came and the mermaid dived back into the water.
The haddock was waiting. "I love you," the haddock said.
"My heart belongs to Stanley," the mermaid said.
"Stanley eats people like you for breakfast."
"I know," said the haddock, sadly.
"Fishwives cook us with rice and call it kedgeree."

When daylight came the mermaid sat upon the rock and
combed her hair while the haddock hung about humbly
where her tail fins touched the foam.
"Go away," the mermaid cried, when she saw
Stanley's boat put out from the shore.
But the haddock would not go.
"*Kedgeree, kedgeree,*" the mermaid hissed.
It was the worst thing that she could think of.

Then Stanley's boat went by and in the stern sat a
bold handsome woman. It was Moll the fishwife
in her best serge skirt, with a bustle.

Moll also fancied Stanley.

Stanley looked at the mermaid, and he looked at Moll.

Moll looked at the mermaid.

"I wouldn't have a tail for all the world," said Moll.

"Not if you *paid* me, I wouldn't have a tail."

The mermaid looked at
Moll's serge skirt
with the bustle.

Next morning when she sat upon the rock she was
fetchingly decked out in an old fishing net.
Round the back, under the net, was a lobster pot.
Stanley brought his boat very close to the rock
and seemed impressed.

The haddock saw the fishing net and when the mermaid
came down that evening he was waiting for her with a
few strands of bladderwrack wrapped round his fins.
"I love you," said the haddock.
"How ridiculous you look," the mermaid said,
and punctured several of the bladders with a fishbone.
The haddock went away and wept bitter tears, but
as they were fifteen fathoms down, nobody noticed.

Next day the mermaid sat upon her rock, fanning
herself with a flounder, and Stanley's boat came nigh.
Stanley stood up in the stern just as the haddock
broke the surface.
"O come with me to the bottom
of the sea," the haddock cried.
"Come instead to my
bonny boat and we'll
be wed," said Stanley.
"Oh, Stanley, yes!"
the mermaid
gasped.

Stanley steered his boat dangerously near
to the rock and the mermaid slithered aboard.
"Don't forget your fishing net,"
said Stanley. He was still worried
about the neighbours.

"Come back, come back," the haddock begged, but at that moment his fins stuck fast in the mermaid's skirt and he was dragged on board behind her.

"I see you've brought our wedding breakfast with you,"
Stanley said, and he whipped out his fish knife.

The haddock raised his fin in a final salute.
"Farewell, beloved. Remember, when you eat
your kedgeree, that you are eating me," he
whispered, and prepared to breathe his last.

At those words the mermaid understood that
she could never be a fishwife. She rose up
on her tail fins and turned on Stanley.
"You brute!" she cried, and hit him in
the eye with her flounder.

Then she seized the haddock in her arms and leaped over the side.

Down below, the mermaid and the haddock
gazed deep into each other's eyes.
"What a blind fool I've been," the mermaid said.
"Can you ever forgive me?"
"I love you," said the haddock.

"Huh! Women!" said Stanley, and turned his
boat for the shore, where Moll was waiting.
"Huh! Fish!" said Moll. "I warned you
about girls like her."

Stanley married Moll and after ten years they had seven children.

But the mermaid and the haddock
had thousands - all at once.

Here are some more picture books published by
Simon & Schuster Young Books for you to enjoy:

There's a Monster Next Door!
Peter Kavanagh
Robby Brown has a problem. He lives next door to a monster. He's not exactly sure
what kind of monster it is, but he's seen its huge hairy hands taking in a parcel and
he's even heard it roaring at night!

Millie's Letter
Frank Rodgers
Millie writes a letter to her dad, who is a sailor on a big ship, reminding him to be
home in time for her birthday. Then, on the night before her birthday, Millie's letter
takes her on a magical journey.

Baby Bear's Nose
Written by Penny McKinlay · Illustrated by Siobhan Dodds
One day Mummy Bear looks at Baby Bear and says, "You've got your daddy's nose!"
Baby Bear is horrified – his daddy has a huge black snout, nothing like his own small
black button nose.

Mole in a Hole
Written by M Christina Butler · Illustrated by Meg Rutherford
In the spring, Bear moves to a cool den near the river. And Mole moves to a cosy hole
in the river bank, right underneath Bear's home. Bear is outraged to find molehills in
his floor, and Mole is furious when Bear steps on his passageways. Will Bear and Mole
learn to become good neighbours?

Available from all good bookshops.
For more information please contact The Sales Department,
Simon & Schuster Young Books, Maylands Avenue, Hemel Hempstead,
Herts HP2 7EZ. Tel: 0442-881900 Fax: 0442-214467.